MAGIC GONE WRONG

Laura Shenton

MAGIC GONE WRONG

Laura Shenton

Iridescent Toad Publishing

Iridescent Toad Publishing.

Cover by Janina Cover Designs.

First edition. ISBN 978-1-913779-57-3

Chapter One

Hannah scooped a generous spoonful of tuna into Toby's chipped ceramic bowl and set it carefully on the worn linoleum of her kitchen floor. The sleek black cat gave an appreciative purr as he brushed against her ankle, his silky fur tickling her skin before he dove enthusiastically into his breakfast. His tail flicked with contentment as he ate, the tip occasionally twitching with pleasure.

"Yeah, yeah, I love you too," Hannah said with a fond smile, scratching between his velvety ears. The rumble of his purr intensified at her touch. "But only when you're not shedding all over my bed and leaving little black reminders of yourself everywhere I go."

Golden morning light filtered through the half-drawn blinds of her modest apartment kitchen area, casting long, peaceful shadows across the countertops and creating a gentle pattern on the tiled backsplash. The air smelt of fresh coffee and the lingering aroma of last night's herbal experiment – a mixture of sage and rosemary that still clung to the walls. Hannah tucked a wayward strand of dark green hair behind her ear and poured herself a cup of coffee from the drip machine that had seen better days but still faithfully produced her morning brew. She'd dyed her naturally brown hair on a whim three months ago during a full moon, and the vibrant emerald colour suited her pale complexion and hazel eyes so well she'd kept it up, despite the maintenance it required. The loose-fitting navy sports hoodie and worn jeans she wore felt comfortable against her skin – practical clothing for a practical witch, nothing flashy or dramatic about her appearance to give away her true nature.

Though 'witch' wasn't exactly how most people in her life would describe her. To her colleagues at Cornerstone Books, the independently owned store tucked between a café and a vintage clothing shop on Maple Street, she was just Hannah Riley, the slightly eccentric assistant manager with an encyclopaedic knowledge of obscure literature and a knack for finding books customers swore they'd couldn't find but were actually wedged behind shelving units or misplaced in entirely wrong sections. They attributed her uncanny abilities to good memory and attention to detail, never suspecting that a whispered locator charm might be involved.

Only Grace knew the full extent of her abilities – the true depth of the power that ran in their bloodline. Hannah specialised in subtle spells, gentle tweaks to fate that helped things fall into place for the people who needed it most. A whispered charm to delay a train by just thirty seconds so a frazzled commuter could make it aboard. A discreet enchantment to make a lost wallet reappear in plain sight for a panicked student. A warmth spell for the elderly neighbour whose heating went out in the dead of winter. Her magic was small but purposeful – acts of kindness woven into the ordinary, unnoticed by most but meaningful to those they touched. It was how she made the world a little softer, one spell at a time.

Hannah stirred a generous spoonful of locally sourced honey into her coffee, watching it dissolve into the dark liquid as she leaned against the counter, her hip against the cool laminate edge. The honey was from Mrs Abernathy's rooftop hives three blocks over – a little magical exchange they had going: protection spells for sweet nectar. Her grandmother had taught her that magic was about balance and reciprocity – that the universe could be bent a little, probabilities shifted to subtly influence outcomes, but never broken beyond the fundamental laws that governed reality. "The moment you start playing god," her grandmother had warned with serious eyes while they collected herbs under a waxing moon, "is the moment the universe starts playing with you."

The sound of a key scraping in the front door made Hannah straighten, her spine suddenly tense. The familiar rhythm of the lock turning meant Grace was home. Hannah felt the prickle of magical energy that always accompanied her sister's presence – stronger than her own, more volatile, like static electricity before a storm.

"Morning, sunshine," Grace called, stepping into the apartment with confident strides. Unlike Hannah, who had inherited their mother's gentle features, round face, and slender build, Grace had their father's height and commanding presence. Her dark hair was pulled back in a practical ponytail that accentuated her sharp cheekbones, and she wore a tailored charcoal blazer over a crimson blouse that screamed 'professional' while still looking effortlessly cool. A silver pendant hung at her throat – protection magic, though Hannah knew it needed recharging more often than Grace bothered with.

"You're back early," Hannah commented, pulling a second cup from the cabinet – the blue one with the chip on the handle that Grace always preferred. "Coffee?"

"God, yes," Grace said, dropping her weathered leather messenger bag on a kitchen chair with a heavy thud that suggested it contained more than just notebooks and pens. Dark circles shadowed her eyes, a testament to her recent schedule. "Been up since four tracking down a lead. My feet are killing me, and I'm pretty sure I've had enough diner coffee to permanently damage something vital."

Hannah handed her sister the steaming cup, catching the familiar scent of Grace's sandalwood perfume mixed with city air. "Another cheating spouse case? The usual trail of hotel receipts and incriminating text messages?"

Grace accepted the coffee with a grateful nod, wrapping her long fingers around the cup for warmth. "I wish. Those are straightforward. Predictable human nature, messy but simple. No, this is house business." She took a long sip, watching Hannah over the rim of her cup with those dark eyes that always seemed to see too much.

Hannah stiffened, her fingers tightening around her own cup. "Which house?" The question came out sharper than she intended, anxiety already rising in her chest.

"Hemlock," Grace said casually, as if she hadn't just named one of the most ruthless witch houses in the city, a family notorious for their approach to magic that skewed towards the toxic and dangerous.

"Are you insane?!" Hannah hissed, setting her cup down with enough force to slosh coffee onto the counter, the dark liquid pooling on the laminate surface. "The Hemlocks? They don't play by anyone's rules, Grace. Not the council's, not the old accords – nobody's."

The city's magical community operated through a complex system of houses – essentially magical families that had grown into political entities over centuries of alliances, feuds, and careful bloodline management. Each had their specialties and territories, their secret libraries and closely guarded grimoires. Hannah and Grace had chosen to remain houseless after their grandmother died, preferring independence to the complicated loyalties and power games that came with house affiliation. Grace had turned her magical sensitivity and investigative skills into a career as a private detective, often taking on cases that involved uncovering dirt on one house for another – a dangerous game of magical politics that kept Hannah awake more nights than she cared to admit.

Grace shrugged with deliberate nonchalance, though Hannah caught the slight tightening around her eyes. "My client has certain assurances in place. The money's good. Very good."

"So is being alive," Hannah retorted, grabbing a dish towel to mop up the spilt coffee. "What are you even investigating? What could possibly be worth the risk?"

"Can't say," Grace said, taking another sip of her coffee, her red lipstick leaving a crescent mark on the cup's edge. "Client confidentiality. You know the rules. But it's solid work, Han. Nothing I can't handle. You know I've built up quite a reputation for discretion."

Hannah felt her frustration mounting, a familiar tension headache beginning to pulse at her temples. "People who cross the Hemlocks tend to disappear. Remember three years ago? That witch – that finder who specialised in locating lost magical artefacts? She took a job looking for something the Hemlocks had apparently stolen, and no one's seen her since."

"That's just rumours," Grace said dismissively, though her eyes darted away, focusing on the calendar hanging lopsided on the refrigerator. "There's no solid proof linking them to any of those disappearances. The council investigated and found nothing conclusive."

"Because the Hemlocks are good at covering their tracks!" Hannah threw her hands up, her voice rising with genuine fear. The lights flickered briefly in response to her emotional surge – a reminder to maintain control. "You know what? I could probably get you a job at the bookstore if you asked. My boss loves you. She's always saying you've got excellent presence whenever you drop by."

Grace laughed, but there was an edge to it, a brittleness. "Shelving books for minimum wage? No thanks. This gig is paying our rent for the next three months – with plenty left over for those concert tickets you've been eyeing. That folk-rock band you're obsessed with – what are they called? The Midnight Hollows?"

"I'd rather have a sister than concert tickets," Hannah said quietly.

Grace's expression hardened, her jawline tightening as it always did when she felt cornered. "I know what I'm doing, Hannah. I've been at this for years. I take precautions. I have contacts. I don't go in blind."

"Like what? Your protection amulet? That thing barely holds a charge!" Hannah pointed to the silver pendant. "I can see the magical signature fading from here. When's the last time you refreshed it? Two weeks ago? Three?"

"I don't need you mothering me," Grace snapped, her voice taking on the cutting edge that appeared whenever Hannah pushed too hard. "I'm the older sister, remember? I was looking out for you when you were still struggling with basic cantrips."

"Then act like it!" Hannah shot back, her fear transmuting to anger in an instant. "Take some responsibility instead of chasing the next adrenaline rush! Is this about the money, or is it about proving something?"

"Is that what you think I'm doing?" Grace's voice rose, the temperature in the kitchen dropping several degrees as her magic reactively cooled the air around them. "While you're hiding in your little bookstore with your little spells, some of us are trying to make a real difference in this city! Some of us aren't content with charming extra dog treats into people's pockets and finding lost books!"

The words hung in the air between them,

sharp and cutting. Hannah felt her cheeks flush with anger and hurt, a lump forming in her throat. Toby had retreated under the table, sensing the magical tension that now crackled between the sisters like invisible lightning.

"Grace, I..." Hannah began, already regretting the escalation, searching for the words that would bridge the sudden chasm between them.

But Grace was already grabbing her bag and heading for the door, the leather strap clutched tightly in her white-knuckled grip. "I've got work to do. Real work."

"Grace, please. I'm worried about you," Hannah pleaded, taking a step forward, her hand outstretched. "This isn't about your abilities. It's about who you're dealing with. The Hemlocks play for keeps."

"Save it," Grace said coldly, her voice carrying a hardness that made Hannah flinch. "I'll be back when I'm back. Don't wait up."

The door slammed behind her with enough force to rattle the framed protection sigil hanging in the entryway, leaving Hannah alone in the kitchen with the lingering tension and a half-full coffee cup rapidly cooling on the counter. The apartment felt suddenly larger and emptier without Grace's presence, the silence oppressive.

Toby meowed softly and rubbed against her legs, his yellow eyes fixed on her with what looked like genuine concern, as if sensing her distress with that quiet, inscrutable awareness that always seemed to linger behind his gaze.

"She's being reckless," Hannah told the cat, who blinked sympathetically, his whiskers twitching. "And she knows it. That's why she got so defensive." She sighed deeply and leaned down to scratch Toby's chin, feeling the soft vibration of his purr against her fingertips. "She'll come around, right? She always does. She just needs to cool off."

But as she moved through her morning routine, brushing her teeth with mechanical movements and selecting a more presentable outfit for her shift at the bookstore, the knot of worry in her stomach refused to dissipate. She applied minimal makeup, just enough to look put-together while her mind remained fixated on Grace. She'd never seen her sister so defensive before, so quick to lash out, and something about this Hemlock investigation already felt different – more dangerous, more secretive than Grace's usual cases.

They had argued before – that was inevitable when two strong-willed witches shared a space – but they'd never parted like this, with such cold, deliberate words designed to wound. They had never gone to bed angry at each other before, an unspoken rule they'd maintained since childhood. Hannah hoped today wouldn't be the first time, but the cold knot of dread in her stomach suggested otherwise.

She tucked her keys and phone into her pocket and grabbed a light jacket from the hook by the door. She took one last look at the empty apartment, at the two coffee cups still sitting on the counter – quiet reminders of the conversation they'd left unfinished – before heading out.

She pulled the door shut behind her, whispering a quick protection charm that settled over the apartment like an invisible web – a small spell, a sister's concern, an echo of something softer Grace might not even notice upon her return.

If she returned.

Chapter Two

Hannah stumbled through her front door at 6:30pm, physically and emotionally drained. The bookstore had been unusually busy, with three separate customers demanding to speak to a manager over trivial matters – one about a slightly dog-eared book being sold at full price, another insisting a bestseller was incorrectly shelved, and the third complaining about the temperature inside the store. Throughout the long, tedious day, her argument with Grace had replayed in her mind, each mental rerun making her feel worse, the harsh words they'd exchanged echoing with increasing volume.

"Grace?" she called, dropping her keys in the ceramic bowl by the door. The metal made a familiar clinking sound against the glazed surface. No answer came from within the apartment.

The living area was quiet, bathed in the stillness that settled when the place felt empty, save for Toby's welcoming meow as he padded towards her, his paws making soft thuds against the hardwood floor. His tail stood straight up, quivering slightly at the tip – a greeting reserved just for her.

"Hey, buddy," she said, scooping him up into her arms. His warm weight against her chest provided immediate comfort, his soft fur brushing against her chin. "Is she not back yet?"

Hannah tried not to worry, though concern had already begun to gnaw at the edges of her mind. Grace often worked late, especially when on a case that had captured her interest or challenged her skills. Still, after their fight earlier that morning, Hannah had hoped her sister would be home so they could talk things out, smooth over the jagged edges of their disagreement.

She fed Toby, the sound of dry food hitting his bowl unnaturally loud in the quiet apartment. She heated up leftover pasta for dinner, the microwave's hum filling the kitchen momentarily. The aroma of tomato sauce and herbs did little to stimulate her appetite, but she forced herself to eat, knowing she needed sustenance. Afterwards, she tried to distract herself with a novel she'd purchased on discount from the store – a mystery she'd been meaning to read for weeks – but the words swam before her eyes, refusing to form coherent sentences. Her eyes kept drifting to the clock on the wall, watching the minute hand make its slow, taunting journey.

7:30pm came and went, the sky outside the window darkening from twilight to night. Then eight, the streets below now illuminated by streetlamps casting pools of yellow light.

By nine, Hannah found herself checking her phone every few minutes, the screen lighting up her immediate line of sight in the dim living area. No messages from Grace. Not even a 'working late' text, which was unusual and increasingly concerning. Grace might be reckless, prone to diving headfirst into situations without considering the consequences, but she was usually considerate about letting Hannah know where she was. It was an unspoken agreement between them, a small courtesy that meant everything in their sometimes-complicated relationship.

At 9:30pm, Hannah called Grace's phone, her fingers trembling slightly as they tapped the screen. It rang several times before going to voicemail, her sister's cheerful recorded voice a stark contrast to her own growing anxiety.

"Hey, it's me," Hannah said after the beep, trying to keep her voice steady despite the worry tightening her throat. "Just checking in. I'm sorry about this morning – about what I said. Call me when you get this, ok? Please?"

By ten, the apartment felt too quiet, too empty, as if even the walls were holding their breath. Hannah paced the living area, her novel abandoned on the coffee table, its bookmark sticking out from between the pages. The floorboards creaked under her feet as she moved, a rhythmic accompaniment to her racing thoughts. When Grace's phone went straight to voicemail on the second call, the knot of worry in her stomach tightened into something closer to dread.

"This isn't like her," Hannah murmured to Toby, who had positioned himself on the arm of the couch, watching with alert yellow eyes that seemed to glow in the dim light. "She always charges her phone. She's practically attached to it."

Her mind began generating scenarios, each more distressing than the last. Mugging. Road accident. Trouble with a case gone wrong. Hannah tried to push these thoughts away, but they persisted, hanging in her mind like dark shadows.

At 10:55pm, as Hannah debated whether to call some of Grace's friends, a strange sensation rippled through the air. It was subtle at first, like the pressure change before a storm, then intensified until it raised goosebumps on her skin. The hair on her arms stood up, electricity seemingly crackling around her. Toby's fur bristled as he hissed at something unseen, his back arching and tail puffing to twice its normal size.

A violet light, soft at first then growing in intensity, shimmered into existence above the kitchen counter, coalescing into glowing letters that hung suspended in the air like neon signs untethered from any surface. Hannah's breath caught in her throat, a small gasp escaping her lips. Violet – the signature colour of Hemlock House, unmistakable to anyone familiar with the witch houses of the city.

The message, written in elegant, swirling script that somehow managed to look both beautiful and threatening, read:

We have your sister. If you contact the council, she dies. If you involve other houses, she dies. Wait for further instruction.

The letters pulsed once, then twice, before dissipating into wisps of smoke that curled and twisted in the air before fading entirely. Hannah stood frozen, her heart hammering against her ribs so violently she thought they might crack under the pressure. The message had been brief, but its implications were devastating, a bomb dropped into the centre of her world. The Hemlocks had Grace, and they were threatening to kill her.

"No, no, no," Hannah whispered, gripping the edge of the counter to steady herself as her knees threatened to buckle beneath her.

The cool surface anchored her to reality when everything else seemed to be spinning out of control. "This can't be happening."

But it was. The lingering scent of violet magic – like lavender mixed with something metallic and sharp – permeated the kitchen area, tickling her nose and leaving a bitter taste on her tongue. This wasn't a prank or a hallucination brought on by worry. This was real, as real as the floor beneath her feet, as real as the fear now coursing through her veins like ice water.

Hannah's mind raced, thoughts tumbling over one another like leaves in a storm. The witches' council would have the resources to help, the authority and power to demand Grace's return, but if the Hemlocks discovered she'd gone to them… it didn't bear thinking about; she couldn't risk Grace's life – not when the threat had been so explicit, so final. And she had no connections with other houses who might be powerful enough to stand against Hemlock, no allies she could call upon in this desperate hour.

"This is my fault," she told Toby, who had jumped onto the counter and was sniffing at the spot where the message had appeared, whiskers twitching as he detected the lingering traces of magic. "I should have stopped her. I knew she'd be in danger being anywhere near the Hemlocks, but I didn't push hard enough."

Guilt and fear threatened to overwhelm her, rising like floodwaters, but Hannah pushed them aside with a deliberate mental effort. Falling apart wouldn't help Grace. Self-recrimination could wait. She needed to focus, to think clearly. She needed a plan.

She took several deep breaths, centring herself as her grandmother had taught her years ago. In through the nose, out through the mouth. Again. And again. Until the panic receded just enough for rational thought to reassert itself.

Her regular magic wouldn't be enough; this realisation settled in her mind with cold certainty. The minor charms she specialised in were useful for everyday annoyances, not for facing off against one of the most powerful witch houses in the city. She needed something stronger, something that could match the Hemlocks' formidable magical arsenal.

Grandmother's grimoire.

The thought came unbidden, rising from some deep recess of her mind, but once it surfaced, Hannah couldn't dismiss it. Her grandmother had been a powerful witch, respected and sometimes feared, affiliated with multiple houses before ultimately choosing independence. Her grimoire contained spells far beyond Hannah's usual repertoire – including some that bordered on forbidden, magic that whispered of ancient powers and forgotten ways.

Hannah hurried to her bedroom, her feet carrying her almost without conscious direction. She dropped to her knees beside the bed and pulled open one of the storage drawers built into the frame. Shuffling past a tangle of scarves and old notebooks, she reached for the leather-bound book tucked at the very back, wrapped carefully in silk cloth the colour of midnight. Her fingers trembled slightly as she lifted it out.

The grimoire was old, its pages yellowed and fragile, its binding worn from generations of use. The leather cover was etched with symbols that shifted subtly when glimpsed from an angle, never quite the same twice. Hannah had never used the more advanced spells it contained, partly out of respect for her grandmother's warnings – "Some knowledge comes with a price" – and partly out of fear. Some of the magic described in its pages required sacrifices she had never been willing to make.

Until now.

She carried the book to the kitchen table, its weight substantial in her hands, and began flipping through it carefully. The pages crackled softly as she turned them, releasing the scent of old paper and dried herbs. Levitation spells, invisibility charms, curses – she scanned each one, evaluating and dismissing them in turn. None seemed powerful enough to stand against an entire house, especially one as established and formidable as Hemlock. Then, about three-quarters through, the pages falling open as if the book itself was guiding her search, she found it: a demon-summoning ritual.

The illustrations were detailed and unsettling – intricate diagrams of summoning circles, symbols whose meanings had been lost to time, and marginalia written in her grandmother's spidery handwriting, cautioning against hasty decisions.

Witches and demons had a complicated relationship, stretching back centuries. Demons possessed power far beyond what most witches could access; summoning one was illegal under council law, punishable by severe sanctions, and for good reason. Demons always demanded payment for their services, and the price was rarely simple or straightforward. Stories abounded of witches who had called upon demonic assistance only to find themselves bound in contracts they couldn't escape, their lives or souls no longer their own.

Hannah stared at the page, tracing the intricate summoning circle with her finger, feeling a slight tingle of dormant magic respond to her touch. It was dangerous. Reckless, even. The very thing she'd probably accused Grace of being that morning during their argument.

But what choice did she have? What other option remained when the stakes were so high?

She thought of Grace – stubborn, brave, infuriating Grace – in the hands of Hemlock House. She imagined her scared, possibly hurt, waiting for rescue that might never come. The image was unbearable, a knife twisting in her heart.

"I have to try," Hannah whispered to Toby, who had followed her to the kitchen area and now sat on a chair, watching her with unblinking eyes that seemed to hold an almost human understanding. "I can't abandon her. Not to them."

With renewed determination, Hannah began gathering the supplies listed in the grimoire. Chalk for the summoning circle – not ordinary chalk, but the special kind infused with ground bones and minerals that she kept hidden in a box beneath her herbs and tea. Seven black candles, thick and unscented, which she'd purchased years ago for a protection ritual but never used. A silver knife, its handle wrapped in leather worn smooth by generations of witches' hands.

The ritual took an hour to prepare, each step completed with meticulous care. Hannah cleared the living area, pushing furniture against the walls to make space for the elaborate chalk pattern on the hardwood floor. The scrape of chair legs and the thud of the coffee table against the wall seemed unnaturally loud in the tense silence. She positioned the candles at specific points around the circle, each placement determined by the phase of the moon and the hour of the night, lighting each one while reciting the phrases her grandmother had phonetically transcribed in the margins. The Latin words felt alien in her mouth, but carried a resonance that made the air vibrate slightly.

When everything was ready – the circle drawn with precise strokes, the candles burning with steady flames that cast long shadows across the space – Hannah stood at the edge of the circle, knife in hand. According to the grimoire, a witch's blood served as both invitation and binding – it would draw the demon to this realm and establish the initial terms of engagement. A contract written in the most personal of inks.

"Here goes nothing," Hannah murmured. The apartment felt uncomfortably warm despite the cool night, the air heavy with anticipation. Before she could reconsider, before doubt could creep back in and weaken her resolve, she pressed the knife into the tip of her finger, hissing as the sharp sting broke the skin. A small bead of blood welled up, dark and rich.

Hannah let it drip onto the chalk lines as she recited the summoning incantation, watching as each crimson drop seemed to be absorbed into the floor, the chalk glowing faintly where the blood touched it. The words of the incantation felt strange on her tongue, ancient and powerful, each syllable carrying weight and intention.

For a moment after she finished speaking, nothing happened. The apartment remained silent except for her slightly ragged breathing and the soft hiss of candle flames. Then, just as disappointment began to creep in, the candles flared simultaneously, their flames stretching impossibly high towards the ceiling, casting the apartment in an eerie, dancing light. The chalk lines began to glow with a pulsing pink light – not like the violet of Hemlock House, but something warmer, almost inviting – that grew brighter with each second until Hannah had to squint against its brilliance.

The air in the centre of the circle shimmered, rippling like the surface of disturbed water. Hannah caught her breath, heart pounding in her chest, as a figure began to materialise within the disturbance. Not the monstrous creature with horns and scales that she'd half-expected from childhood stories and pop culture depictions, but a tall, slender man with skin so pale it seemed to glow from within, luminescent like moonlight on fresh snow. He had high cheekbones that could cut glass, red eyes that somehow managed to look kind despite their demonic nature, and short, neatly styled black hair with elegant sideburns framing his face. He wore what appeared to be an impeccably tailored three-piece suit that wouldn't have looked out of place in a period drama – charcoal grey with subtle pinstripes, complete with a waistcoat and a pocket watch chain that glinted gold in the candlelight.

He was beautiful in an otherworldly way, his features too perfect to be human, and Hannah found herself momentarily transfixed, unable to look away from this creature that had answered her desperate call.

The demon surveyed the apartment with a casual grace, taking in the hastily pushed-aside furniture, the flickering candles, and finally Hannah herself, his gaze lingering on her face as if reading her thoughts. His lips curved into a smile that might have been friendly, almost charming, if not for the pointed teeth it revealed, sharp and white as new ivory.

"Well," he said, his voice unexpectedly warm and cultured, carrying the faintest hint of an accent she couldn't quite place. "It's been a while since I've been called to this realm. Decades, at least." He adjusted his cuffs, an oddly human gesture for a being of such power. "What can I do for you, witch? What desperation brings you to summon one such as me?"

Hannah opened her mouth to respond, to explain about Grace and the Hemlocks and her desperate need for help against forces that outmatched her. But before she could speak, before the first word could leave her lips, a black blur streaked across the apartment with startling speed. Toby, sensing a threat to his mistress or perhaps responding to some feline instinct to protect, launched himself at the demon with a ferocious yowl that sounded nothing like his usual meow – deeper, almost primal.

"Toby, no!" Hannah cried, lunging forward instinctively though she knew she couldn't reach him in time. Her foot stopped just short of crossing the chalk line, a barrier she dared not breach while the ritual was active.

It was too late anyway. The cat and demon collided in mid-air, and a blinding flash of pink magic filled the apartment, so bright it seared Hannah's vision. She shielded her eyes with her arm, feeling the surge of power wash over her like a wave, prickling her skin and making her hair stand on end. The air crackled with electricity, and the scent of ozone mixed with something sweeter, like burnt sugar.

When the light faded and she could see again, spots dancing in her vision, Hannah gasped in shock. The demon's human form was gone, dissipating into wisps of pink smoke that curled and twisted before vanishing completely. And Toby – her familiar, her companion, her ordinary housecat – was sitting calmly in the centre of the circle, looking thoroughly confused. His yellow eyes blinked rapidly, and his tail twitched in agitation.

"What just..." Hannah began, then froze as Toby opened his mouth.

"Well," said the cat in a deep, melodious voice that was decidedly not feline, the same cultured tones that had emerged from the demon's lips moments before, "this is unexpected."

Chapter Three

Hannah stared at Toby – or rather, at the demon now inhabiting Toby's body – with a mixture of horror and disbelief. The black cat sat perfectly still in the centre of the chalk circle, its posture unnaturally erect, yellow eyes gleaming with an intelligence that had never been there before. The faint scent of magic still hung in the air, a lingering reminder of the ritual that had gone so terribly wrong.

"You're... in my cat," she finally managed, her voice barely above a whisper. Her fingers trembled as she clutched the edge of her grandmother's worn oak bookshelf for support.

The cat tilted his head, yellow eyes blinking thoughtfully. The movement was deliberate, calculated – nothing like Toby's usual playful mannerisms. "It appears so," the demon replied in that same rich, cultured voice that was entirely at odds with his feline form. "Your familiar attacked as I was attempting to exit the summoning circle. Quite brave of him, if rather ill-advised. Most creatures instinctively sense danger and flee. Yours chose to protect you instead."

The sound of human speech emerging from her pet's throat sent shivers down Hannah's spine. She sank to her knees on the hardwood floor, still keeping a cautious distance from the circle. The chalk lines glowed with a faint pink luminescence, casting eerie shadows across the dim room.

"Is Toby ok? What's happened to him?" Her heart pounded with guilt. Toby had been by her side since her eighteenth birthday – loyal, protective, hers. Now he'd paid the price for her desperate gambit.

"Your familiar is unharmed," the demon assured her, lifting one paw to examine it with fastidious attention. "Think of him as... sleeping. His consciousness has been temporarily displaced to make room for mine." The cat's tail swished in what might have been irritation, sweeping across the chalk dust. "I, on the other hand, seem to be stuck in this rather limiting form, leaving me tethered to this realm. Most inconvenient."

"Can you change back?" Hannah asked, her mind racing through the limited demonology she'd studied. The candles surrounding the circle flickered despite the absence of any breeze, their flames dancing in response to the magical currents still lingering in the air. This wasn't how the summoning was supposed to go. The grimoire had said nothing about possession. She'd followed every instruction meticulously, double-checking each sigil and incantation.

The cat – demon – attempted to stretch, then looked down at his paws with evident distaste. His tail flicked in apparent frustration. "Not at present. This is... unusual. In all my centuries of being summoned, I've never encountered this particular scenario before."

Hannah pressed her palms against her temples, trying to think clearly despite the surreal situation. The coolness of her silver rings offered little comfort against her flushed skin. "This is a disaster," she murmured, glancing at the grimoire still open on the table, its yellowed pages covered in cryptic symbols and warnings she should have heeded. "I needed your help, and now you're stuck in my cat's body, and Toby is..."

"As I said, your familiar is fine," the demon interrupted, whiskers twitching with impatience. "And I may still be able to help you, depending on what you require." He padded closer to the edge of the circle, moving with a grace that was decidedly un-catlike, each step measured and deliberate. The pink glow intensified where he approached the boundary. "What was so urgent that you resorted to demon summoning, witch? It's not exactly a common practice in this modern age. Most of your kind have abandoned such... traditional methods in favour of your collective councils and circles."

Hannah hesitated, anxiously biting her lower lip. Could she trust this demon? She had no guarantee that he would help her, especially given the unexpected turn the summoning had taken. But what choice did she have? The message from Hemlock House had been explicit in its threats, the violet lettering burning itself into her mind every time she closed her eyes.

"My sister has been kidnapped," she said finally, the words catching in her throat. "By Hemlock House. They sent me a magical message saying they'll kill her if I go to the council or any other houses." The admission made the situation feel even more real, the weight of it pressing down on her shoulders like a physical burden.

"Hemlock," the demon-cat mused, settling into a sphinx-like position, front paws extended before him. "Yes, they've always been a particularly... ambitious group, known for their ruthlessness. What did your sister do to attract their attention?"

"She's a private detective," Hannah explained, shakily tucking a strand of green hair behind her ear. "She was investigating them for another client. Grace has always been too stubborn for her own good – too confident in her ability to handle anything that comes her way."

"I see." The cat's tail flicked thoughtfully, curling around his haunches in a perfect arc, the light catching the subtle sheen of his black fur. "And you summoned me because...?"

"I need help rescuing her," Hannah said, rising slowly to her feet. Her knees protested after kneeling on the hard floor. "My magic isn't strong enough to go against an entire house, especially one as powerful as Hemlock. Their manor is warded against conventional magical approaches, and they have at least a dozen fully trained witches at their disposal."

The demon-cat considered this, yellow eyes narrowing to calculating slits. "A rescue mission. Interesting. And what are you prepared to offer in exchange for such assistance? Demonic aid comes at a price, as your grimoire surely warned."

The question caught Hannah off guard. In her panic, she'd been aware of some of the potential implications of summoning a demon, but hadn't fully considered what she was willing – or even able – to offer in return. She had acted so hastily that she hadn't stopped to think about what the demon might demand as payment. She glanced nervously at the protective amulet hanging around her neck – a gift from her grandmother, which now seemed woefully inadequate.

"I... I'm not sure," she admitted, fingers reaching unconsciously to touch the smooth pendant. "I think I'm prepared to offer whatever is necessary... within reason." The last part came out in a whisper, betraying her fear of what such an offer might entail.

"Indeed." The cat's mouth seemed to curl into something resembling a smile, revealing the tips of sharp white teeth. "However, our current situation complicates matters. I find myself inconveniently housed in feline form, unable to access my full abilities. The parameters have shifted considerably from a standard summoning contract."

Hannah took a slow breath, her mind racing. The stakes were certainly unusual, but a feeling of dread still lingered, making her fear that she would never have the upper hand in any bargain. She couldn't afford to let her guard down.

The demon-cat paced the edge of the circle, tail swishing with increasing agitation. Each step was precise, testing the boundaries of his magical confinement with evident curiosity. "Perhaps we can help each other," he suggested, stopping to face Hannah directly. "I will assist you in rescuing your sister from Hemlock House, and in return, you will help me find a way to return to my proper form. Does that seem fair? A mutually beneficial arrangement rather than the traditional bargain."

Hannah frowned, crossing her arms protectively over her chest. The apartment suddenly felt colder. "How do I know I can trust you?"

"A fair concern," the demon-cat acknowledged with a slight dip of his head. "But consider our positions. I am currently trapped in your familiar's body, with limited access to my powers. You need assistance that requires abilities beyond your own. Neither of us has much choice but to trust the other, at least temporarily. Our interests are, for the moment, perfectly aligned."

He had a point. And Hannah was running out of options and time. Every minute that passed was another minute Grace remained in Hemlock's grip. The house wasn't known for their patience or mercy. The violet message had made it clear they wouldn't hesitate to eliminate a problem if it became too much.

"Fine," she said at last, squaring her shoulders with newfound determination. "But if you try to trick me, or if you harm my sister or Toby in any way..."

"Yes, yes," the demon interrupted, waving a paw dismissively. "You'll curse me to the depths of whatever humans currently believe lies beneath. I understand. Such threats are tedious but expected. Rest assured, I have no interest in harming you, your sister, or your familiar. The latter would be particularly counterproductive given my current accommodation."

Hannah took a deep breath, her gaze travelling around the small apartment that had always been her sanctuary. Now it felt different – charged with an energy that hadn't been there before. With a decisive motion, she stepped forward and broke the chalk line of the summoning circle with her foot. The pink glow faded with a soft hiss.

"There," she said, her voice steadier than she felt. "You're free to move about, but remember our deal. I'm trusting you because I have no choice, not because I want to."

The cat stretched languidly, arching his back in a way that seemed both feline and somehow not, then delicately stepped out of the circle. His paws left faint pink impressions on the floor that faded after a few seconds. "Splendid," he said, looking around the apartment with evident curiosity. "Now, shall we introduce ourselves properly? I am Millian, Third Demon of the Seventh Realm."

"Hannah," she replied automatically, then mentally kicked herself for not thinking to use a pseudonym. Names had power in magical dealings – another lesson from her grandmother.

"A pleasure," Millian said, giving a small bow that looked absurdly formal coming from a cat. "Now, Hannah, why don't you tell me everything you know about your sister's disappearance and Hemlock House's involvement? The more information I have, the better I can assist you. Details matter greatly in such delicate operations."

Hannah nodded and moved to the kitchen table where she'd left her grandmother's grimoire. Millian followed, leaping gracefully onto the tabletop to see the book. His paws sounded lighter than usual as he landed, another reminder that this was not truly Toby moving around her apartment.

"I don't know much," Hannah admitted, sinking into a chair and running her fingers along the worn leather binding of the grimoire. "Grace was investigating them, but she wouldn't tell me the details. Said it was confidential. This morning we argued about it – I told her it was too dangerous." She swallowed hard, fighting back tears at the memory of Grace brushing off her concern, all confident and defensive as though nothing could touch her. "Then tonight I got this message."

She described the violet lettering that had appeared above her kitchen counter – how it had shimmered into being like floating neon, pulsing brighter until the message took shape. How the words had hovered in the air, untethered to any surface, glowing with the unmistakable signature of Hemlock House. The threat, the warning, and the chilling instruction to wait for further contact.

"Classic intimidation tactics," Millian observed, settling into a seated position, his tail curling neatly around his paws. "They want you anxious and compliant. Fear makes witches remarkably malleable. But the fact that they bothered to contact you at all is interesting. If they simply wanted your sister eliminated, they wouldn't have sent a message."

"So she's alive?" Hannah asked, hope flaring in her chest. She leaned forward, hands gripping the edge of the table so tightly her knuckles whitened.

"Almost certainly," Millian confirmed, his tone matter-of-fact but with what might have been a hint of kindness. "They're using her as leverage, which means they want something from you. Dead hostages serve no purpose except as warnings, and they've made no indication that this is their intent."

The relief that flooded through Hannah made her feel weak. She ran a hand through her green hair, disturbing the careful waves she'd styled that morning in what felt like another lifetime.

"Thank god," she whispered, closing her eyes briefly to compose herself. Then, more composed: "But what could they possibly want from me? I'm not anyone important in the magical community. I work in a bookstore. I practice small magic – humble spells, minor compassion, nothing that would interest a house like Hemlock."

Millian regarded her with those uncanny yellow eyes, his gaze uncomfortably perceptive. "Perhaps it's not about who you are, but what you can do. Or what you have access to. Hemlock has always had a particular interest in ancient knowledge and artefacts. They collect power through acquisition."

Hannah frowned, her gaze drifting around her small apartment with its mismatched furniture and walls covered in botanical prints. "I don't have access to anything valuable. Unless…" A thought struck her, cold realisation washing over her. "Unless they know about Grandmother's grimoire."

"A powerful witch's grimoire would certainly be a prize worth kidnapping for," Millian agreed, his gaze dropping to the ancient book between them. "Especially if it contains rare or forbidden spells. Family grimoires often preserve knowledge that has otherwise been lost to time."

Hannah looked down at the ancient book, its pages yellowed with age, the margins filled with her grandmother's handwriting adding commentary to spells that dated back centuries. "Like demon summoning?"

"Precisely." Millian's whiskers twitched thoughtfully. "Such knowledge has become increasingly rare in your world. Modern witches prefer cleaner, safer magic. Summoning has fallen out of favour, deemed too dangerous and unpredictable. Even witches who have knowledge of, or interest in, demon summoning are always eager to learn different versions of how such rituals can be performed. Indeed, beyond demon-summoning, your grandmother's grimoire holds significant value for the diverse range of ancient magic it covers. Any witch looking to enhance their powers would surely regard it as an asset."

They lapsed into silence as Hannah processed this new possibility. If Hemlock House was after her grandmother's grimoire, they would be disappointed. She'd never give up the family heirloom, especially not to a house that had kidnapped her sister.

"So what do we do?" she finally asked, absently gazing at the grimoire.

Millian's ear twitched at a sound Hannah couldn't hear. "We wait for their next contact. In the meantime, we prepare. Hemlock House will expect a lone, frightened witch. They won't be expecting you to have... unusual assistance. Surprise is a powerful advantage, particularly when confronting an overconfident opponent."

Hannah looked sceptically at the demon-possessed cat, taking in his small stature and delicate build. Toby had always been more sleek than muscular. "No offence, but you're not exactly intimidating like this. Toby weighs eight pounds soaking wet. How much help can you really be?"

"Appearances can be deceiving," Millian replied, a hint of amusement in his voice. "Even in this form, I have access to some of my abilities – I can feel it with absolute certainty. Not as many as I'd like, but enough to be useful. Power does not always manifest as physical strength."

To demonstrate, he focused on Hannah's empty coffee cup on the table. His eyes narrowed in concentration, pupils expanding until they nearly consumed the yellow irises. The ceramic began to glow with a soft pink light, then levitated several inches above the surface before gently settling back down. The display was small but precise, showing fine control rather than raw power.

"That's... helpful, I guess," Hannah said, not entirely convinced. She'd expected something more impressive.

"It's a start," Millian conceded, looking slightly winded from the effort. "But I believe I can access more of my power once I become better acquainted with this form. Physical vessels require adaptation. And you, my dear witch, have magic of your own. Together, we might just be formidable enough to challenge Hemlock House."

Hannah still had her doubts, but Millian's confidence was somewhat reassuring. And really, what other options did she have? Going to the council was out of the question, and she didn't know anyone in the magical community with the strength or influence to stand against Hemlock.

"Alright," she said, closing the grimoire with a decisive thud. "We'll wait for their instructions, but we'll be ready when they come." She ran a hand through her hair, suddenly aware of how exhausted she felt. The argument with Grace, the stress of the day, the summoning ritual, and now this bizarre partnership with a demon-possessed cat – it was all too much.

Tears welled in her eyes, catching on her lashes before she could blink them away, and before she could stop them, they were rolling down her cheeks. Everything had gone so terribly wrong. Grace was in danger, Toby was possessed, and she had no idea if she was making things better or worse.

To her surprise, Millian approached her, his movements careful and deliberate. The light scratch of his claws against the tabletop was oddly comforting in its ordinariness. He sat down in front of her and reached out one black paw, the gesture strangely formal and dignified despite coming from a cat.

"We will fix this," he said, his voice gentler than before, the cultured tones softened with what might have been genuine sympathy. "Both your sister's situation and my... accommodation issue. You have my word. And contrary to popular belief, some of us do honour our promises."

Hannah looked at the extended paw, then at the demon's face – Toby's face, but with an unmistakably different presence behind the yellow eyes. The familiar features were arranged in an expression her cat had never worn – solemn, determined, and oddly reassuring. Could she really trust him? Did she have any choice?

She reached out and gently touched his paw in a symbolic handshake, feeling the soft pads against her fingertips. The contact sent a strange tingling sensation up her arm – not unpleasant, but definitely magical.

"Ok," she said softly, wiping away her tears with her free hand. "We have a deal."

Chapter Four

Hannah jerked awake to a strange humming in the air – low, resonant, and vibrating through her bones. A violet glow bloomed just above the coffee table, pulsing softly like a heartbeat. Disorientated, she blinked several times, the fog of sleep refusing to lift as quickly as she needed it to. She'd fallen asleep on the couch, sometime after three in the morning, she assumed, following hours of worry and ruminating.

Now, golden light streamed through the blinds, catching on the swirling motes of dust that danced in the sunbeams. It was late morning, but the peaceful hush in the room was a lie.

She sat up, her breath catching in her throat as the glow intensified, coalescing into floating letters that shimmered in the air above the table – violet and unmistakable. The same magic as before, from no other than Hemlock House.

The words formed in elegant, threatening script:

Your grandmother's grimoire: bring it to Blackwater Park, north entrance, noon today. Come alone.

The letters pulsed once... twice... before dissolving into violet smoke, the wisps curling into the still air until they vanished completely.

Hannah's heart slammed against her ribs. This was it – contact from Grace's captors. She swallowed hard, her mouth dry as dust, and called out, "Millian!"

The sleek black cat emerged from the kitchen, moving with the effortless grace that seemed exaggerated now that she knew the creature inhabiting Toby's body wasn't just feline. Despite having been summoned and finding himself in an unfamiliar body, Millian looked infuriatingly composed, his yellow eyes sharp in the morning light.

"They've made contact," Hannah said, her voice unsteady. "Another message. Same magic as before."

Millian leapt onto the couch beside her, his gaze settling on the empty space where the message had hovered only moments before. "Blackwater Park," he observed, his voice incongruously deep and cultured coming from the cat's small body. "Isolated enough to avoid witnesses, but public enough that they won't attract attention from other magical entities. Clever."

"And you were right; they want the grimoire," Hannah confirmed. The ancient book felt suddenly heavier on her lap, its worn leather cover warm beneath her fingers. She had fallen asleep holding it, conscious that it was coveted by witches willing to stoop low to obtain it. "What's our plan?"

After discussing several options the previous night, debating strategies until Hannah's eyes had grown heavy with exhaustion, they had settled on a two-pronged approach: Hannah would appear to comply while Millian, using what demonic powers he could access in cat form, would create a diversion if needed.

"The plan remains the same," Millian said, his tail swishing slowly back and forth, betraying a tension that his measured voice concealed. "You'll bring the grimoire – or rather, a convincing replica – while I scout the location ahead of time."

Hannah nodded and hurried to get ready, her mind racing with possibilities and contingencies. After a quick shower that did little to wash away her anxiety, she dressed in practical clothing: her most comfortable jeans, sturdy hiking boots that would allow her to run if necessary, and her favourite navy sports hoodie that felt like armour against the world. She tied her hair back in a tight ponytail, not wanting anything to obstruct her vision or provide an easy handhold for an enemy, then set about creating their decoy grimoire.

The previous night, Millian had taught her a simple illusion spell that would make an ordinary notebook appear identical to her grandmother's grimoire. The spell had taken her three attempts to master, leaving her fingers tingling with residual magic. The illusion wouldn't hold up to intense magical scrutiny, but it might buy them enough time to locate and rescue Grace before the deception was discovered.

"Remember," Millian said as they prepared to leave, the real grimoire safely hidden under Hannah's mattress between layers of protective wards and the fake one securely tucked in her backpack, "Hemlock could have at least three witches present – one to verify the grimoire, one to guard your sister, and one to handle any... complications."

"You mean to kill me if anything goes wrong," Hannah said grimly, her stomach clenching at the thought. The Hemlock House witches weren't known for their mercy or forgiveness.

"Precisely," Millian confirmed, his yellow eyes unblinking. "Which is why I'll be watching from a hidden position. If things go south, I'll create a distraction. Your job is to protect yourself and get to Grace. Are we clear?"

Hannah nodded, adrenaline and determination pushing aside her fear like a physical force. "Crystal."

***

As she made her way to the bus stop, Hannah's backpack felt unnaturally light in the absence of a genuine grimoire's considerable weight. She figured Millian would be way ahead of her by now, perhaps eagerly scouting Blackwater Park already. A strange sense of unease settled over her at the thought of Toby's body – so used to naps on windowsills and warm laundry piles – now padding vulnerably through the city streets. He had always been a strictly indoor cat, content to watch the world through glass rather than venture into it. Seeing him – or rather, the demon inhabiting him – step beyond the threshold of the front door like it was nothing had felt surreal.

The park was a fifteen-minute bus ride away, on the eastern edge of the city where the urban landscape gradually gave way to more verdant terrain. Once a private estate belonging to one of the city's founding families, it had been converted to public land decades ago, though parts of it remained wild and rarely visited – perfect for clandestine meetings of all sorts.

As Hannah approached the north entrance, she scanned the area for any sign of Grace or the Hemlock witches, her eyes darting from person to person, searching for threats. The entrance consisted of an imposing stone archway, its weathered grey surface etched with subtle symbols that most visitors would mistake for decorative carvings but that Hannah recognised as ancient wards – magical protections that had stood for centuries. The archway led to a winding path that disappeared into a copse of maple trees, their leaves tinged with subtle colour shifts that caught the light. The air was warm, a lingering heat that clung to her skin and made the shaded path ahead feel invitingly cool.

Few people were around – a jogger stretching nearby, his earbuds firmly in place and his attention focused elsewhere; an elderly couple feeding the ducks at a distant pond, tossing breadcrumbs with methodical precision; and a woman walking a golden retriever that strained eagerly on its lead, oblivious to the tension humming through the park's atmosphere.

None of them gave Hannah a second glance as she passed through the archway and followed the path into the trees, the gravel crunching softly beneath her boots. The air felt different here – heavier, charged with a subtle energy that made the hair on the back of her neck stand up and sent a familiar tingle down her spine. Protective wards, likely placed by Hemlock to ensure privacy and deter mundane visitors from wandering too close to their meeting spot.

About fifty yards in, the path opened onto a small clearing with a weathered stone bench positioned beneath the spreading branches of an ancient oak tree. A woman sat there, her back ramrod straight and her hands folded neatly in her lap. She wore an elegant violet pantsuit that seemed out of place in the rustic setting, the fabric clearly expensive and custom-tailored to her slender frame. Her silver hair was pulled into a tight bun so severe it looked painful, not a single strand out of place. She looked to be in her sixties, with fine lines etched around her mouth and eyes, but her eyes – sharp, calculating, and a startling shade of violet – held the wisdom and cold assessment of someone far older.

"Hannah Riley," the woman said, her voice smooth and cultured, carrying easily across the clearing without seeming to rise above conversational volume. "Right on time. I am Eliza Hemlock."

Hannah's breath caught in her throat, a chill running down her spine despite the warmth of the day. Eliza Hemlock was not just any member of Hemlock House – she was its matriarch, rumoured to be one of the most powerful witches in the city. For her to handle this exchange personally spoke volumes about the importance of it.

"Where's my sister?" Hannah demanded, stopping several feet away from the bench, careful to maintain distance and a clear path to retreat if necessary. Her hands clenched into fists at her sides, nails digging crescents into her palms.

Eliza smiled thinly, the expression never reaching her violet eyes. "Safe, for now. I assume you've brought what we requested?" Her gaze flicked to Hannah's backpack with unconcealed interest.

"I want to see Grace first," Hannah insisted, her voice steadier than she felt. Sweat trickled down her back beneath her hoodie, but she maintained eye contact with the formidable witch before her.

The older witch's eyes narrowed, a flicker of annoyance crossing her otherwise composed features. She nodded, then made a subtle gesture with her right hand – what looked like a casual wave, but which Hannah recognised as a simple summoning spell. From behind a large maple tree stepped two figures: a tall man – another Hemlock witch, Hannah presumed – wearing a violet suit cut from the same expensive cloth as Eliza's, his dark hair slicked back from a severe face; and Grace, her hands bound in front of her with glowing violet cords that hummed with magical energy.

Grace looked exhausted, with dark circles like bruises under her normally bright eyes and her immaculately styled hair in disarray. Her usually crisp blouse was wrinkled and stained, and she stood with a slight hunch that suggested physical discomfort. But she appeared otherwise unharmed, and when she saw Hannah, her eyes widened with a blend of relief and alarm.

"Hannah!" she called out, her voice cracking slightly. "You shouldn't have come! They want..."

"Silence," the male witch said sharply, flicking his fingers in a quick, practiced motion. Grace's voice cut off abruptly mid-sentence, though her mouth continued to move frantically, forming words that produced no sound. A silencing spell, efficiently and cruelly applied.

Hannah took an instinctive step towards her sister, fury building inside her at the sight of Grace's bound hands and silenced voice, but Eliza raised a hand, palm outward in a clear command to halt. "The grimoire first," she said, her tone making it clear this was not a negotiation.

Swallowing her anger and forcing herself to stick to the plan, Hannah slowly removed the fake grimoire from her backpack, feeling the weight of Eliza's gaze on her every movement. As she did, she reached out with her magical senses, trying to locate Millian's presence. She couldn't see him among the dense foliage surrounding the clearing, but she felt a faint tingle of demonic energy somewhere to her left, hidden among the trees and undergrowth. The sensation was reassuring, like having a secret weapon waiting in reserve.

"Here," she said, holding out the book, its cover convincingly aged and marked with the same symbols as her grandmother's true grimoire thanks to Millian's spell. "Now release my sister."

Eliza motioned to the male witch, who approached Hannah with measured steps, his eyes never leaving her face as if expecting a trap. He took the grimoire from her hands, his fingers brushing against hers momentarily – cold as ice despite the warm day. He returned to Eliza's side and opened the book, examining its pages with a critical eye, his fingers tracing over the text and diagrams with attention to detail.

For a tense moment, no one spoke. Hannah held her breath, hoping the illusion would hold under scrutiny, acutely aware of every second that passed. Birds called in the trees above them, their cheerful songs a surreal counterpoint to the tense standoff below. The male witch flipped through several pages, occasionally murmuring under his breath as he tested the book with small detection spells that made the air around him shimmer slightly.

Finally, he looked up at Eliza and gave a slight nod, his expression revealing nothing. Eliza smiled as she took the book from him, a small satisfied curve of her thin lips that didn't soften her cold eyes in the slightest.

"Well done, Miss Riley," she said, closing the book and placing it carefully on the bench beside her. "Your grandmother's grimoire is impressive. Many of these spells would be frowned upon by the council. You can trust that Hemlock house will treat them with the reverence they deserve."

"I don't care about any of that," Hannah said, her voice tight with barely contained emotion. "I care about my sister. Release her, now." She could feel her own magic responding to her agitation, tingling at her fingertips, ready to be called forth if needed.

Eliza studied Hannah for a moment, her violet eyes seeming to look through her rather than at her, then nodded to the male witch. "Release the binding spell, Victor."

Victor waved a hand in a dismissive gesture, and the glowing cords around Grace's wrists disappeared with a faint violet shimmer.

However, she remained frozen in place, her expression frustrated as she tried to speak, the silencing spell still clearly in effect.

"And the silencing spell," Hannah insisted, taking another step forward, her patience wearing dangerously thin.

"In due time," Eliza said, raising one perfectly manicured hand in a placating gesture. "First, there is another matter to discuss. Your sister was investigating certain... activities of our house. Activities that should remain private. We need assurance that both of you will remain silent about what she discovered."

Hannah's mind raced through possibilities. Whatever Grace had uncovered must be significant – perhaps even dangerous. It fuelled her suspicion that the Hemlock matriarch herself was handling this exchange, rather than delegating it to subordinates, because it was something of deep importance.

"Fine," Hannah agreed, trying to keep her voice neutral despite the hammering of her heart. "Neither of us will speak of it. To anyone. Just let her go."

Eliza's smile remained calculating and cold. "I'm afraid verbal assurance isn't sufficient in this case. We'll need a binding oath. From both of you."

Hannah tensed, her muscles coiling like springs. Binding oaths in the magical community were serious business – breaking one could result in anything from loss of magical ability, to excruciating pain, to death, depending on the terms. Once sworn, they were nearly impossible to circumvent.

"What are the terms?" she asked cautiously, buying time while she assessed their options.

"Simple," Eliza replied, her tone suggesting she was offering a reasonable compromise rather than a magical contract that could ruin their lives. "You will not speak, write, or communicate in any way about what Grace discovered regarding Hemlock House. Should you attempt to do so, your magic will be blocked, resulting in the permanent loss of your abilities."

Loss of magic. For a witch, it was almost worse than death – a cutting off from an essential part of oneself, like losing a sense or a limb. Hannah glanced at Grace, who was shaking her head frantically despite the silencing spell, her eyes wide with warning.

"And if we refuse?" Hannah asked, though she already suspected the answer. The temperature in the clearing seemed to drop several degrees despite the warm sunshine filtering through the leaves overhead.

"Then this pleasant meeting ends much less pleasantly," Eliza said, her voice hardening like ice forming on a pond. "And your sister's investigative career comes to a permanent end." The threat hung in the air, all the more chilling for its calm delivery.

Hannah took a deep breath, steadying herself and weighing their limited options. They needed to get out of this situation alive first; they could figure out the rest later. Sometimes retreat was the wisest strategy.

"I'll take the oath," she said, forcing conviction into her voice. "Remove the silencing spell so Grace can agree too."

Eliza nodded to Victor, who flicked his fingers towards Grace in a casual reversal of his earlier spell. Immediately, Grace gasped as her voice returned, taking a deep breath as if she'd been underwater.

"Don't do it, Hannah!" she cried, her voice raw with urgency. "You don't know what they're planning! They're…"

Victor raised his hand again, his eyes narrowing dangerously, but before he could recast the silencing spell, a piercing yowl cut through the clearing like a siren. All heads turned as a black streak shot from the bushes directly towards Eliza Hemlock, moving faster than seemed possible for a normal cat.

Millian, playing his part perfectly.

The cat leapt onto Eliza's lap with supernatural force, hissing and clawing furiously, his yellow eyes glowing with an unnatural light. Startled, the Hemlock matriarch let out a cry of alarm, her carefully maintained composure shattering as she tried to dislodge the furious feline from her expensive pantsuit. Victor immediately diverted his attention to helping her, reaching to grab the furious cat with both hands, his own spell forgotten.

"Hannah, run!" Grace shouted, taking advantage of the chaos to break free from her captors, shoving past the distracted Victor with surprising strength. She sprinted towards Hannah, grabbing her hand and pulling her towards the trees. "This way!"

The sisters raced towards the dense woods, away from the maintained path, branches whipping at their faces and undergrowth catching at their ankles. Behind them, Hannah heard Eliza shouting orders, her cultured voice now sharp with rage, and the sound of pursuit crashing through the underbrush, twigs snapping and leaves rustling.

"We need to split up," Grace said, panting as they ran, her breathing laboured from her captivity. She ducked under a low-hanging branch and pulled Hannah around a dense thicket. "I'll lead them away. You circle back to the north entrance."

"No!" Hannah protested vehemently, tightening her grip on her sister's hand. "I'm not leaving you again!"

"Trust me," Grace insisted, her eyes fierce

with determination as she briefly halted their headlong flight behind the cover of a massive oak tree. "I know these woods better than they do. I've been mapping them for weeks as part of my investigation. Meet me at the east pond in fifteen minutes."

Before Hannah could argue further, Grace veered sharply to the right, deliberately stepping on a dry branch that cracked loudly under her weight and rustling through a patch of dense bushes to attract their pursuers' attention. Hannah hesitated for a split second, torn between following her sister and trusting her plan, then continued straight ahead, moving as quietly as possible, placing each foot carefully to minimise noise.

She heard Victor shout, "That way!" followed by the sound of multiple people following Grace's more obvious path. Hannah pressed on, her heart hammering in her chest, her breath coming in controlled gasps as she navigated through the trees, ducking under branches and weaving between trunks.

After several minutes of careful navigation through the increasingly dense woods, Hannah reached a small stream that she knew would lead towards the east pond. She paused to catch her breath behind a large boulder, her back pressed against the cool stone as she listened intently for any sounds of pursuit. Hearing nothing immediate, she reached out with her senses, trying to locate Millian's distinctive energy signature.

A rustling in the bushes nearby made her freeze, her fingers instinctively forming the first gesture of a defensive spell, but it was only the black cat, looking somewhat dishevelled – his normally sleek fur standing on end in places – but otherwise unharmed.

"Millian!" she whispered in relief, her tense shoulders relaxing slightly. "Are you ok?"

"A few claw wounds on their precious matriarch should keep Hemlock House occupied for a while," he replied, looking rather pleased with himself as he sat and began to fastidiously lick one paw. "I must say, feline claws are quite effective weapons. Though I could have done far more damage in my true form." His yellow eyes gleamed with suppressed power and what might have been frustration at his current limitations.

"We need to get to the east pond," Hannah said anxiously. "Grace is meeting us there."

Millian's ears perked up, swivelling attentively. "Your sister escaped?"

"Yes, she's leading them away from us."

"Clever girl," Millian said approvingly, his tail swishing with interest. "Let's not waste her diversion."

They made their way towards the east pond, Hannah moving as quietly as possible while Millian scouted ahead, his superior senses alert for any danger. The trees grew thicker here, the undergrowth more tangled, but Millian seemed to know exactly which way to go, leading Hannah along game trails too narrow for human hunters to easily follow. The sounds of pursuit seemed distant now, concentrated in another part of the park where Grace was presumably still leading the Hemlocks on a wild chase.

When they reached the small, secluded pond, its surface glittering in dappled sunlight that filtered through the canopy above, there was no sign of Grace. The pond was peaceful, surrounded by reeds and water lilies, a pair of dragonflies skimming across the surface – nature undisturbed by the magical conflict unfolding in the park.

"She'll be here," Hannah reassured herself, trying to ignore the knot of worry forming in her stomach. "She said she knows the area."

Millian leapt onto a moss-covered boulder at the pond's edge, his keen eyes scanning the surrounding trees, his whiskers twitching slightly as he processed sensory information beyond Hannah's capabilities. "Movement," he said suddenly, his entire body tensing. "Northeast corner, approaching fast."

Hannah tensed, readying a defensive spell, her fingers moving into position and her mind recalling the specific words she would need, but relaxed when Grace emerged from the trees, breathless but triumphant, her hair wild and her clothes smudged with dirt and plant material.

"Lost them," she said, still panting, hurrying to Hannah's side. "Led them through the bramble patch on the western ridge. They'll be picking thorns out of their fancy suits for hours." Despite her obvious exhaustion, her eyes gleamed with satisfaction. "But they won't be far behind for long. We need to..." She stopped abruptly, staring at Millian, who remained perched regally on the boulder. "Since when does Toby follow you to the park? And why is he sitting like that?" Her investigator's instincts were clearly triggered by the cat's uncharacteristic behaviour.

Hannah and Millian exchanged glances, a moment of silent communication passing between them.

"It's... complicated," Hannah said, brushing leaves from her sister's shoulder. "I'll explain later. Right now, we need to get out of here."

Grace looked suspicious, her eyes narrowing as she glanced between Hannah and the unusually poised cat, but nodded. "There's a maintenance exit on the far side of the pond. It leads directly to Ashton Street." Her practical nature asserted itself, prioritising escape over immediate explanations.

They set off immediately, Grace leading the way with confident familiarity, Hannah close behind and Millian bringing up the rear, occasionally glancing back to check for pursuers, his ears swivelling to catch any sounds of approach. They reached the maintenance gate without incident – a small metal door set into the park's boundary wall, partially concealed by a thick curtain of ivy that Grace pushed aside to reveal the rusted lock.

Grace produced a small key from her pocket. "Copied it months ago when I was investigating a cheating spouse who liked to use this exit for his afternoon liaisons," she explained with a hint of her usual professional pride. The lock turned with a reluctant squeak of protest.

Once through the gate, they found themselves in a quiet residential area, the neat rows of townhouses a stark contrast to the wild park they'd just escaped. Grace hailed a passing taxi with a practiced whistle, and minutes later, they were heading away from Blackwater Park, the vehicle's air conditioning a welcome relief after their woodland flight.

"Our apartment is compromised," Hannah said quietly, aware of the driver's potential curiosity. "They know where we live."

"I have somewhere safe in mind," Grace replied, her voice equally low. "A client's place – I know I shouldn't take advantage of it like this, but he's away on a business trip all month. There's no way Hemlock will know anything about it – it's linked to a nice, simple, human case."

Hannah nodded, relieved that her sister's professional habits were proving useful. She glanced down at Millian, who sat calmly on her lap, his eyes half-closed in a convincing performance of feline disinterest, playing the role of ordinary cat for the taxi driver's benefit.

84

Chapter Five

Twenty minutes later, Hannah, Grace and Millian arrived at a modest brownstone in a quiet neighbourhood – the sort of area where neighbours minded their own business and asked few questions. Grace led the way down a narrow side path to a basement apartment, unlocking the door with another key from her seemingly endless collection, this one attached to a small imitation rabbit's foot keychain, worn smooth from use.

The apartment was small but clean, furnished simply with a worn but comfortable-looking couch, a coffee table bearing several water ring stains, a compact kitchenette with the basics, and a single bedroom visible through an open door. The windows were small, positioned high on the walls near the ceiling, providing limited light but also limited visibility from outside – perfect for their current needs.

Once inside with the door locked and heavy curtains drawn across the windows, Grace turned to Hannah, crossing her arms across her chest. "Ok, what the hell is going on? How did you find me? And why is Toby acting weird?"

Hannah took a deep breath, running a hand through her ponytail, which had become increasingly dishevelled during their escape. "You might want to sit down for this."

As Hannah explained everything – the violet message that had appeared in their apartment, her desperate decision to summon a demon despite the risks, and the bizarre accident that led to Toby's possession – Grace's expression shifted from scepticism to shock to a sort of grudging admiration. She sat on the edge of the couch, leaning forward with her elbows on her knees, interrupting occasionally with sharp questions that revealed her investigator's mind working overtime.

"So... our cat is now possessed by a demon named Millian," Grace summarised when Hannah finished, eyeing the black cat who had made himself comfortable on a cushion, his tail wrapped neatly around his paws. "And you made a deal with him to help rescue me."

"That's correct," Millian said, causing Grace to flinch visibly despite the prior explanation. Hearing a human voice emerge from the familiar cat was evidently more disconcerting than the abstract knowledge that it could happen.

"That is so weird," Grace muttered. "My sister's cat is talking to me. With a pleasantly cultured accent, no less."

"Technically, I'm a demon currently occupying your sister's cat," Millian corrected with a hint of irritation. "A situation I'm not particularly thrilled about, but here we are."

Grace ran a hand through her tangled hair, wincing as her fingers caught in a knot. "And you gave the Hemlocks a fake grimoire?"

Hannah nodded, sinking onto the couch beside her sister. "An illusion spell Millian taught me. It won't fool them for long, though. Once they try to actually use any of the spells, they'll realise the text is just an illusion over blank pages."

"Clever, but certainly a short-term solution," Grace agreed grimly. "When they realise what you've done, they'll be furious." She looked at Hannah, her expression suddenly serious. "Do you have any idea what you've done? The real reason they wanted that grimoire?"

"For the powerful spells?" Hannah guessed, suddenly uncertain. "Grandmother's grimoire contains some pretty advanced magic."

Grace shook her head, her expression grim. "It's much worse. The Hemlocks are planning a coup against the council. They've been gathering artefacts and spells to strengthen their position for months. Grandmother's grimoire was on their list because it contains a ritual they need – something about binding the power of other houses."

Hannah's breath caught in her throat, her eyes widening as the implications sank in. "How do you know this?"

"That's what I was investigating," Grace explained, lowering her voice despite their relative safety. "A council member hired me to find evidence of the Hemlocks' plan. I thought the house would be distracted during one of their gatherings, so I broke in, hoping – expecting – not to be noticed. But I got careless – overconfident – and they caught me photographing documents in Eliza's private study."

Millian's ears perked up with interest, his yellow eyes gleaming. "A coup against the witches' council? Ambitious, even for the Hemlocks."

"It gets worse," Grace continued, her expression darkening further. "The binding ritual they're looking for – it involves demon magic."

"I think I know the one you mean," Millian said, his tail flicking with idle precision as if to underscore his certainty. "It's a complex ritual that would temporarily bind a demon's power to amplify a witch's abilities – certainly not something to be indulged in lightly."

"That's what they want," Grace said, her voice tight with urgency. "With that kind of power boost, they could overwhelm the council's defences."

The implications sank in like a stone in water, rippling outward. If the Hemlocks succeeded, they could reshape the entire magical community under their control. Given their reputation for ruthlessness and their disdain for those they considered lesser practitioners, it would be disastrous for countless witches.

"Well, they don't have the real grimoire," Hannah pointed out, trying to find a positive angle. "And we're not going to give it to them."

"No, but now they'll be hunting us even more aggressively," Grace said, her lips pressing into a thin line. "We're obstacles to their plans."

Millian stretched languidly on his cushion, his movements graceful. "Not to mention, they now have evidence that you, Hannah, are familiar with demon summoning. That alone makes you a person of interest – especially since demon magic is exactly what they're trying to harness."

Hannah sank deeper into the couch, the weight of their situation settling on her shoulders like a physical burden. The enormity of what they were facing – not just personal danger but a threat to the entire magical community – left her momentarily speechless.

"So what do we do now?" she finally asked, her voice smaller than she intended.

"We need to warn the council," Grace said firmly, her investigator's determination shining through her exhaustion.

"But the binding oath..." Hannah started, worry creasing her brow.

"We never actually took it," Grace reminded her, a spark of her usual confidence returning. "And even if we had, this is bigger than us. The entire magical community is at risk. The council needs to know."

Hannah hesitated, biting her lower lip. Going to the council meant explaining everything – including her illegal demon summoning, an act that carried severe penalties in the magical world. She could face censure, binding, even the stripping of her magical abilities. The thought made her stomach twist with anxiety.

Millian, sensing her concern, raised his head from the cushion and spoke up. "If I may offer a suggestion? You need to resolve two problems: the Hemlock threat and my... accommodation issue. Perhaps they can be addressed simultaneously."

Both sisters looked at him curiously, Grace's eyes narrowing with the intensity she usually reserved for particularly complex situations.

"I've been considering my situation," Millian continued, his cat body impossibly dignified despite the absurdity of their circumstances. "Hannah, my essence is currently bound to this feline form through an accidental magical convergence – your summoning spell interacting with your familiar's protective instinct. Breaking this bond would likely require a significant magical event."

"Like what?" Hannah asked, leaning forward with interest, a strand of green hair falling across her face.

"Like disrupting the Hemlocks' plan," Millian proposed, his tail twitching with what might have been excitement. "If they are attempting a major magical working involving demon energy, and we were to interfere at a critical moment, the resulting magical backlash could be sufficient to break the connection tethering me to your familiar."

Grace looked sceptical, her investigative cynicism written clearly across her features. "You're suggesting we let the Hemlocks get close to completing their coup attempt, then sabotage it at the last minute? That's incredibly risky."

"All the best plans are," Millian replied with what appeared to be a smirk, whiskers twitching with amusement. "Besides, we have advantages they might not be expecting – namely, me. Even in this limited form, I can sense and manipulate demonic energies better than any witch. It's my native realm, after all."

Hannah considered the proposal, turning possibilities over in her mind. It was dangerous, fraught with potential for disaster, but it might be their best chance to both stop the Hemlocks and restore Toby to normal. Sometimes the most direct approach was best, as her grandmother had often told her.

"We'd need to know exactly what they're planning and when," she said, already trying to break the problem into manageable pieces. "And we'd need a way to counter their magic at the critical moment."

"The 'when' part is easy," Grace said, shifting into the familiar territory of investigation planning. "It would have to be during the full moon three nights from now. The Hemlock files I accessed mentioned preparations for an 'ascension' on that date."

"And the 'where'?" Hannah asked.

"There's an old stone circle in the northwest corner of Blackwater Park," Grace said, her voice taking on a precise tone. "It's on ley lines that amplify magical workings. I found references to it in the Hemlock files I was investigating. The stones themselves date back centuries."

Millian nodded approvingly, his whiskers twitching. "Good. As for countering their magic, I can guide you in preparing the necessary spells. With my knowledge and demonic energies, we should be able to craft something effective. The key will be timing and precision."

Hannah looked at Grace. "What do you think?"

Grace sighed, massaging her temples with her fingertips. "I think it's risky, but I don't see many alternatives. We can't go to the council without evidence – they'd just arrest you for summoning a demon and disregard our warnings as an attempt to distract from your own crime. And we can't just hide and hope the Hemlocks give up. They're not the type to walk away from a plan once it's in motion."

"So we're doing this?" Hannah asked, a mixture of fear and determination in her voice.

"We're doing this," Grace confirmed with a resigned but resolute expression. "God help us."

Millian stretched again, his feline body arching elegantly, radiating satisfaction despite his physical limitations. "Excellent. As for the real grimoire – retrieving it physically is out of the question now that your apartment is compromised. I'll use my powers to suspend it in a pocket realm, safely out of reach. No one will be able to touch it, not even me, until the three of us all agree otherwise." He flicked his tail, eyes gleaming. "Now, this place is as safe as any for the time being. We should stay put while we plan. We haven't got long, and there's much to prepare."

Chapter Six

Three nights later, Hannah crouched behind the dense undergrowth at the edge of the small clearing in Blackwater Park. The cool night air carried the earthy scent of damp soil and vegetation, sending a slight shiver down her spine. Beside her, Grace kept watch, her posture tense but determined, while Millian – still trapped in Toby's body – sat alert between them, his feline form almost unnaturally still in the shadows of the foliage.

The ancient stone circle at the centre of the clearing consisted of seven weathered megaliths arranged around a flat altar stone. Each monolith stood like a silent sentinel, their rough surfaces etched with the passage of centuries. The night was clear, with countless stars scattered across the velvet expanse above, and the full moon – swollen and luminous – bathed everything in an ethereal silvery light that made the stones seem to glow from within.

"They're late," Grace whispered, checking her watch with a nervous glance. Her fingers tapped anxiously against her thigh. "It's almost midnight."

"They'll come," Millian replied quietly, his cat eyes reflecting the moonlight in eerie amber pools. "They won't squander this opportunity."

As if summoned by his words, soft footsteps approached from the main path. Hannah's heart quickened as she peered through the lattice of leaves to see a solemn procession of violet-robed figures entering the clearing. She counted seven in total – a magically significant number that sent a chill of recognition through her – with Eliza Hemlock leading the way. The matriarch's imperious face still bore faint scratches from Millian's attack days earlier, the marks standing out against her pale skin like accusatory fingers.

The Hemlock witches arranged themselves around the stone circle with authoritative precision, each taking position by one of the towering megaliths. Their movements were fluid and synchronised, betraying years of ritual practice together. Eliza stood at the altar stone, her hair catching the moonlight as she unfolded what appeared to be an ancient parchment, its edges crumbling with age.

"Remember the plan," Millian murmured, his voice barely audible above the gentle rustle of leaves. "We wait until they begin channelling the demon energy. That's when the barrier between realms will be thinnest and our counter-spell will have maximum effect. Any earlier, and we risk failure; any later, and they may gain control of powers beyond our ability to counter."

Hannah nodded, her hand tightening around the small cloth bag containing the components for their disruption spell. The fabric felt soft against her palm, belying the potent mixture within. She and Millian had spent the past three days meticulously crafting it, drawing on his demonic expertise.

Grace touched her arm reassuringly, her fingers warm against Hannah's chilled skin.

The sisters had reconciled fully during their preparation, with Grace apologising for her recklessness and Hannah acknowledging her overprotectiveness. The tension that had stretched between them had finally eased, replaced by a deeper understanding and respect. Whatever happened tonight, they would face it together, their shared blood and magic stronger than any threat.

In the clearing, Eliza began to chant in an ancient language that made the air vibrate with power. The syllables seemed to hang in the space between sound and silence, each word pulsing with intent and meaning. The other witches joined in, their voices blending in perfect harmony to create a resonance that grew in power with each repetition. Violet energy, like liquid lightning, began to pulse between the stones, forming a translucent dome over the circle. The temperature around Hannah dropped noticeably as the magic drew energy from the surrounding environment.

"They don't have the real ritual from your grandmother's grimoire," Millian observed, his whiskers twitching with analytical interest. "They're using a substitute – less efficient, but still potentially effective. Notice how the energy fluctuates instead of flowing smoothly? They're compensating with brute force rather than precision."

The chanting intensified, the words coming faster and the voices rising in volume until they seemed to press against Hannah's skin like a physical presence. The violet energy coalesced into a swirling vortex above the altar stone, spinning with increasing velocity. Through its turbulent centre, Hannah glimpsed what appeared to be another realm – a place of shifting shadows and strange lights that seemed to follow laws of physics differently from their own. Colours she had no names for flickered at the edges of her vision.

"They're opening a portal to the demon realm," Millian said, his voice tense with recognition. His feline body quivered with suppressed energy. "This is it. They'll attempt to draw power through without complete control. Their arrogance will be their undoing."

Hannah readied the disruption spell, her fingers tingling with anticipation and her own magic responding to the charged atmosphere. According to their painstakingly crafted plan, she would cast it at the precise moment when the Hemlocks began to channel demonic energy, causing a controlled magical backlash that would disrupt their ritual and – hopefully – break the connection binding Millian to Toby without causing catastrophic damage to the fabric of reality itself.

The vortex widened, its edges rippling like disturbed water. Tendrils of crackling red energy began to stream through, intertwining with the violet magic of the Hemlock witches. The air filled with the sharp tang of ozone and something else – a sulphurous undertone that made Hannah's nose wrinkle. Eliza raised her hands, her face exultant and transformed by the otherworldly light as she began to draw the demonic power into herself. Her eyes glowed with an unnatural intensity, and her voice rose above the others in triumphant command.

"Now!" Millian hissed, his tail lashing decisively.

Hannah stood in a single fluid motion and

hurled the spell component – a meticulously balanced mixture of herbs, crushed crystals, and a small vial containing a drop of her own blood to bind it to her intent – directly into the centre of the vortex. At the same moment, she spoke the words of power that Millian had taught her, ancient syllables that felt both foreign and strangely familiar on her tongue. She felt the magic surge through her with unprecedented force, rushing from the earth beneath her feet, through her body, and out through her extended hands in a torrent of raw potential.

The effect was immediate and dramatically spectacular. The spell component exploded in a blinding burst of emerald-green light as it hit the vortex, creating a cascade of magical dissonance that reverberated through the clearing like silent thunder. The carefully structured violet energy of the Hemlock ritual shattered like glass under the impact, fracturing into a thousand glittering shards, and the demonic power they had been attempting to harness backlashed violently in a wave of crimson fury.

Eliza screamed – a sound of rage rather than fear – as the magical feedback knocked her backward with such force that she slid several feet across the moss-covered ground. The other witches staggered as if physically struck, their perfect circle broken and their concentration shattered. Some fell to their knees, while others struggled to maintain their footing. The vortex began to collapse in on itself, spinning wildly and throwing off sparks of conflicting energies that hissed and spat when they touched the ground.

Beside Hannah, Millian's feline form suddenly convulsed, his back arching impossibly high. A pink glow enveloped him, pulsing in time with the collapsing vortex and growing brighter until Hannah had to shield her eyes against its intensity. The air around them hummed with the sound of reality reconfiguring itself. When she looked again, Toby lay on the ground, his small feline body unconscious but seemingly unharmed, his chest rising and falling in a peaceful rhythm as though he were fast asleep. A few feet away, the tall, elegant figure of Millian in his true form was materialising, still translucent but rapidly solidifying as if being painted into existence by an invisible hand.

"It's working!" Hannah cried, exhilaration coursing through her veins. "Grace, get Toby!"

Grace darted forward with practiced agility to scoop up the unconscious cat, cradling him protectively to her chest, while Hannah maintained the counter-spell with outstretched hands, sweat beading on her brow as she forced the collapsing vortex to remain stable enough for Millian to fully manifest. The effort made her arms tremble and her vision swim, but she held firm, drawing on reserves of strength she hadn't known she possessed.

In the stone circle, the Hemlock witches were regrouping with remarkable speed, their initial shock giving way to trained discipline. Eliza, her immaculate robes now stained with dirt and moss, rose to her feet, her face contorted with rage that transformed her features into something almost bestial. She pointed directly at Hannah, her finger trembling with barely contained fury.

"You!" she snarled, her voice raw with hatred. "I should have known! Destroy her! Leave nothing but ash!"

Three of the witches turned towards Hannah, raising their hands in unison to cast offensive spells. Violet energy gathered at their fingertips, crackling ominously in the night air. But before they could release their deadly assault, Millian stepped forward, now fully materialised in his demon form, his presence commanding immediate attention. The witches faltered, their expressions shifting from determined anger to uncertain fear as they recognised what stood before them.

"I believe," Millian said, his cultured voice carrying easily across the clearing despite its soft tone, "that you were attempting to harness power from my realm without proper invitation or safeguard. An ambitious endeavour, but also a flagrant violation of rules you well know. The council might have something to say about that – assuming my kin don't seek redress first."

As if on cue, bright lights suddenly illuminated the clearing from all sides, cutting through the darkness like physical entities. Figures in ceremonial robes of the witches' council emerged from the trees in a co-ordinated movement, their staffs glowing with containment spells that hummed with suppressive energy. Their faces were hidden beneath deep hoods, but their authoritative presence was unmistakable.

"Eliza Hemlock," announced a commanding voice from the tallest figure, "you and your coven are charged with attempting forbidden magic and conspiring against the council. The evidence of your transgression stands before us all. Surrender your powers temporarily and come peacefully, or face immediate binding."

Hannah stared in shock as the council witches moved in to arrest the Hemlock group, expertly containing their attempts at resistance with spell-dampening restraints. She turned to Grace, who was gently cradling Toby against her shoulder, a small smile playing at the corners of her mouth.

"Did you...?" Hannah began, realisation dawning.

Grace smiled sheepishly, a glint of her old mischievous self breaking through her recent trauma. "I may have sent an anonymous tip to a council contact – with just enough evidence to get them here tonight, but not enough to implicate us in any... creative interpretations of magical law."

"You brilliant, sneaky..." Hannah began with admiration, but was interrupted by Millian approaching them, his footsteps silent on the ground despite his substantial presence.

In his true form, the demon was even more striking than Hannah remembered – tall and elegant, with pale skin that seemed to glow from within like alabaster lit by a hidden flame. His features were perfectly proportioned, beautiful in a way that transcended human standards, and those same kind red eyes that had first captured Hannah's attention now gazed down at her from a face framed by neatly styled black hair and elegant sideburns. He still wore the charcoal three-piece suit she remembered, its subtle pinstripes catching the light, the gold of his pocket watch chain glinting faintly beneath the moonlight. Existing in feline form, it seemed, hadn't changed him one bit; here stood a demon with all the dignity he had commanded when Hannah had first summoned him that night in the apartment.

He bowed formally to the sisters, the gesture carrying centuries of courtly grace. "Ladies, I believe our business is concluded. Grace has been rescued, the Hemlock threat is no more, and I am restored to my proper form. A successful venture all around, wouldn't you agree?"

Hannah looked at Toby, who was beginning to stir in Grace's arms, his whiskers twitching as consciousness returned. "Is he ok?" she asked nervously.

Millian nodded, his expression softening. "Your familiar will be fine. A bit confused, perhaps, with some unusual dreams for a feline mind to process, but he has suffered no lasting harm. My possession was careful, despite the unexpected circumstances."

Relief flooded through Hannah, washing away the last of her adrenaline and leaving her suddenly aware of her exhaustion. "Thank you," she said sincerely, meeting those strange red eyes without fear. "I know this wasn't what either of us planned when I performed that summoning, but... I'm grateful for your help. I'm sure that not all demons would have been as honourable."

"The feeling is mutual," Millian replied with unexpected warmth. "This has been one of my more interesting visits to your realm in recent centuries. Most summonings are so predictably tedious – vengeance and petty power grabs." He glanced at the council witches, who were busy securing the Hemlocks with magical bindings that glowed blue in the moonlight. "However, I should depart before they turn their attention to me. Demons – even helpful ones – are not precisely welcome at council proceedings. Such is the bureaucracy of these things."

"Will you be able to return to your realm?" Grace asked, adjusting her hold on the increasingly squirming Toby.

"Yes," Millian confirmed with a casual gesture towards the dissipating magical energies. "The disruption spell created a temporary pathway that lingers even now. I can use it to return home without difficulty." He hesitated, then added with a slight tilt of his head, "Though perhaps not immediately."

Hannah raised an eyebrow, curiosity overcoming her weariness. "What do you mean?"

"I find myself somewhat… intrigued by your city," Millian admitted, his gaze drifting towards the distant lights visible through the trees. "It's been such a long time since I last got to explore this realm, and much has changed. The pace of human innovation is remarkable. I might do some sight-seeing before going home – sample your cuisine, visit your museums, perhaps even take in what you call a 'film'."

"Just don't possess anyone else's pets," Grace warned, though her tone was light and her eyes sparkled with tentative humour. "Some might not be as understanding as we were."

Millian chuckled, the sound rich and melodious. "I assure you, that's not something I plan on doing. Feline senses are overwhelming, and the dietary restrictions are most inconvenient. I prefer my own form, with all its capabilities intact."

In the distance, one of the council witches called out to another, their voices suggesting they were finishing their work with the Hemlocks and might soon widen their investigation to the surrounding area.

"That's my cue," Millian said, straightening his already perfect posture. "I think we can all agree it's time for the grimoire to return to its rightful place under your bed, Hannah. I'll make sure it's there for you when you get back to your apartment."

"Thank you again for helping us," Hannah said. "It has made all the difference in so many ways."

"You're more than welcome." He bowed once more, the gesture somehow both theatrical and entirely sincere. "Hannah Riley, it has been a pleasure. Your grandmother would be proud of your resourcefulness and courage. If you ever require demonic assistance again…" he smiled, revealing those pointed teeth that should have been frightening but somehow weren't, "…perhaps try a different summoning location. One with more expansive accommodations."

Before Hannah could respond with more than a startled laugh, Millian stepped back into the lingering traces of magical energy from the collapsed vortex. There was a flash of pink light, brief but intense, and then he was gone, leaving behind only a faint scent of something both musty and herbal, with a lingering warmth in the air where he had stood.

"We should go too," Grace said urgently, her practical nature reasserting itself. "Before the council start asking questions about the counter-spells performed in the vicinity."

Hannah nodded, and they slipped away through the trees, moving as quietly as their hurried departure would allow. Grace carried Toby in her arms. Though he seemed disorientated, occasionally stopping to shake his head as if trying to dislodge confusing thoughts, they trusted Millian's word that the faithful feline would be fine.

Chapter Seven

Back at their apartment, Hannah collapsed onto the couch, the events of the night finally catching up with her in a wave of bone-deep fatigue. Every muscle ached with the aftermath of magical exertion, and her mind felt fuzzy around the edges. Grace brought her a steaming cup of chamomile tea with a touch of honey – their grandmother's recipe for magical depletion – and sat beside her, their shoulders touching in comfortable companionship. Toby, seemingly recovered from his ordeal, curled up in Hannah's lap, purring contentedly as if nothing unusual had happened, though his eyes occasionally darted to empty corners of the room as if tracking invisible movements.

"Wow," Grace said after a moment of peaceful silence, cradling her own cup in her hands. "I still can't believe you summoned a demon to save me."

Hannah smiled tiredly, running her free hand through her tangled hair. "You investigated a dangerous witch house despite my warnings. I think we're even on the recklessness scale."

"Fair enough." Grace sipped her tea thoughtfully, the steam rising to soften her features. "What happens now? The Hemlocks will be facing council justice, but they know you summoned a demon. That's not exactly something the magical community takes lightly."

"I'm not worried," Hannah replied, surprising herself with the truth of the statement. "With what the Hemlocks were trying to do, no one's going to believe anything they say about us. Besides, the grimoire is safe, you're safe, Toby's back to normal..." She shrugged one shoulder. "I'd call that a win, wouldn't you? We can figure out the rest as it comes."

Hannah noticed her sister looking at her with newfound respect.

"You've changed, you know," Grace said. "A week ago, you wouldn't have dreamed of breaking magical laws or confronting a powerful witch house. You were always the one telling me to play it safe."

Hannah stroked Toby's fur absently, considering this observation. The cat arched into her touch, his purrs deepening. "I did what I had to. When it really matters, the rules have to bend. I don't regret it." She paused, taking a sip of her tea before adding, "Though maybe next time you take on a dangerous case, I'll just come with you instead of staying home to worry myself sick. We work better as a team than I realised."

Grace laughed, the sound lighter than it had been in days, and clinked her cup against Hannah's in a gesture of solidarity. "I'll drink to that." She raised her cup higher in a proper toast.

Hannah smiled and clinked her cup against Grace's once more. "And to magic gone wrong that somehow ended up right."

Outside, the full moon continued its arc across the sky, casting a soft glow over the city. Hannah looked out of the window, her gaze lingering on the distant rooftops. She imagined Millian somewhere out there, wandering the streets with his usual air of elegant curiosity, taking in the sights of the city in his leisurely exploration. She wondered how he'd find the bustling crowds, the unfamiliar sounds, and the dizzying pace of modern human life – so different from the realm he'd come from. It seemed odd, in a way, that a being of such power and dignity would be intrigued by something as mundane and ordinary as the city, but endearing too.

Her thoughts shifted, and a quiet gratitude filled her chest. Out of all the demons that could have been summoned, she'd been incredibly fortunate to end up with Millian. He had been nothing like the monstrous beings she'd been warned about, the ones that wreaked havoc and left destruction in their wake. Millian had helped them, guided them, and had shown a surprising level of honour and respect. In the chaos of the summoning, she had never imagined that the outcome would be this good.

Hannah shifted her gaze from the window to Toby, his obsidian fur gleaming softly in the dim light of the room. She watched him for a moment, the rhythmic rise and fall of his chest a quiet reassurance. He was no longer the unwitting vessel for Millian's power, no longer caught between worlds. He was just Toby, her familiar, the cat who had been with her through thick and thin.

A warm smile tugged at the corner of her lips. She had never fully appreciated how much his presence meant to her until now, when everything felt like it had come full circle. Even if he did insist on getting fur everywhere, she would cherish him all the more for it. After all, what were a few extra cat hairs in exchange for the loyalty, companionship and quiet comfort he provided?

Hannah savoured the silence of the moment. All the danger and uncertainty of the past week had come to an end. Things were back to normal. As normal as they could be, at least. She thought back to her earlier fear – that everything would fall apart, that she'd lose Grace, that she'd never feel safe again. But she had faced that fear, and survived it. And in the process, she had learnt so much about herself. Her confidence with magic had grown, not from any newfound power, but from knowing that even when things went wrong, she had the strength to confront them.

In the quiet of the room, with Toby curled up on her lap and Grace sitting next to her, Hannah realised that perhaps she truly had everything she needed. Enough to live a life where, going forward, she would stick to using only the subtle magic she was used to, tucked away for the little things. Helping someone in need, easing a small burden, or brightening a dark day; nothing grand – just the humble, everyday magic that made the world a little gentler. That was all she wanted now.

And with that thought, she closed her eyes, feeling a deep, abiding gratitude for everything she had, everything that was still to come. The world might be full of unexpected twists and turns, but for now, she was content.

For now, everything was exactly as it should be.